Dear Parent:
Your child's love of reading starts here!

Every child learns to read in a different way and at his or her own speed. Some go back and forth between reading levels and read favorite books again and again. Others read through each level in order. You can help your young reader improve and become more confident by encouraging his or her own interests and abilities. From books your child reads with you to the first books he or she reads alone, there are I Can Read Books for every stage of reading:

SHARED READING
Basic language, word repetition, and whimsical illustrations, ideal for sharing with your emergent reader

BEGINNING READING
Short sentences, familiar words, and simple concepts for children eager to read on their own

READING WITH HELP
Engaging stories, longer sentences, and language play for developing readers

READING ALONE
Complex plots, challenging vocabulary, and high-interest topics for the independent reader

ADVANCED READING
Short paragraphs, chapters, and exciting themes for the perfect bridge to chapter books

I Can Read Books have introduced children to the joy of reading since 1957. Featuring award-winning authors and illustrators and a fabulous cast of beloved characters, I Can Read Books set the standard for beginning readers.

A lifetime of discovery begins with the magical words "I Can Read!"

Visit www.icanread.com for information
on enriching your child's reading experience.

For information address HarperCollins Children's Books,
a division of HarperCollins Publishers,
195 Broadway, New York, NY 10007
www.icanread.com

ISBN: 978-0-06-257221-9

Manufactured in Dong Guan City, China
Lot#:

17 18 19 20 21 SCP 5 4 3 2 1
06/17

I Can Read!™

ADVENTURES OF FRANCES

by Russell Hoban
Pictures by Lillian Hoban

HARPER

An Imprint of HarperCollinsPublishers

Table of Contents

Bread and Jam for Frances
Page 7

Best Friends for Frances
Page 45

A Baby Sister for Frances
Page 83

A Birthday for Frances
Page 121

for Julia,
    who likes to practice
    with a string bean
    when she can

BREAD AND JAM
FOR FRANCES

by Russell Hoban
Pictures by Lillian Hoban

It was breakfast time.

Father was eating his egg.

Mother was eating her egg.

Gloria was sitting in a high chair
and eating her egg too.

Frances was eating bread and jam.

"What a lovely egg!" said Father.

"It is just the thing to start the day
off right," said Mother.

Frances did not eat her egg.

Frances sang a little song to it.

She sang the song very softly:

I do not like the way you slide,

I do not like your soft inside,

I do not like you lots of ways,

And I could do for many days

Without eggs.

Frances spread jam

on another slice of bread.

"Why do you keep eating
bread and jam," asked Father,
"when you have a lovely egg?"
"I like bread and jam," said Frances,
"because it does not slide off
your spoon in a funny way."

"Well, of course," said Father.

"But there are other kinds of eggs."

"Yes," said Frances.

"But sunny-side-up eggs

lie on the plate and look up at you.

And sunny-side-down eggs

just lie on their stomachs and *wait*."

13

"I think it is time for you
to go to school now," said Mother.

Frances picked up her books,
her lunch box, and her skipping rope.
Then she kissed Mother and Father
good-bye and went to the bus stop.

While she waited for the bus

she skipped and sang:

   Jam on biscuits, jam on toast,

   Jam is the thing that I like most.

   Jam is sticky, jam is sweet,

   Jam is tasty, jam's a treat—

   Rasp*berry,* straw*berry,* goose*berry,*

   I'm *very*

   FOND . . . OF . . . JAM!

That evening for dinner

Mother cooked breaded veal cutlets,

with string beans and baked potatoes.

"Ah!" said Father. "What is there

nicer on the plate and tastier to eat

than breaded veal cutlet!"

"It *is* a nice dish," said Mother.

"Eat up the string bean, Gloria."

Frances looked at her plate and sang:

> *What do cutlets wear*
>
> *Before they're breaded?*
>
> *Flannel nightgowns? Cowboy boots?*
>
> *Furry jackets? Sailor suits?*

Then Frances spread jam
on a slice of bread and took a bite.
"She won't try *anything* new,"
said Mother to Father.
"Well," said Frances,
"there are many different
things to eat,
and they taste many different ways.
But when I have bread and jam
I always know what I am getting,
and I am always pleased."

"You try new things
in your school lunches," said Mother.
"Today I gave you
a chicken-salad sandwich."
"I traded it to Albert," said Frances.
"For what?" said Father.
"Bread and jam," said Frances.

The next morning at breakfast

Father sat down and said,

"Now I call that a pretty sight!

Fresh orange juice

and poached eggs on toast."

Frances began to sing a little song:

> *Poached eggs on toast,*
>
> *Why do you shiver*
>
> *With such a funny little quiver?*

Then she looked down and saw

that she did not have a poached egg.

"I have no poached egg," said Frances.

"I have nothing but orange juice."

"I know," said Mother.

"Why is that?" said Frances.

"Even Gloria has a poached egg,

and she is nothing but a baby."

"You do not like eggs," said Mother.

"Have some bread and jam

if you are hungry."

So Frances ate bread and jam

and went to school.

When the lunch bell rang

Frances sat down next to her friend Albert.

"What do you have today?" said Frances.

"I have a cream cheese-cucumber-

and-tomato sandwich," said Albert.

"And a hard-boiled egg and salt shaker.

And a thermos of milk.

And a bunch of grapes.

And a tangerine and a cup custard.

What do you have?" he said.

Frances opened her lunch.

"Bread and jam," she said.

"You're lucky," said Albert.

"That's just what you like."

"I had bread and jam

for dinner last night," said Frances,

"and for breakfast this morning.

I am a very lucky girl, I guess."

Albert took a napkin

and tucked it under his chin.

He arranged his lunch neatly.

"I *like* cream cheese with cucumber

and tomatoes on rye," said Albert.

With his spoon he cracked the egg.

He sprinkled salt on the yolk.

He took a bite of sandwich,

a bite of egg, and a drink of milk.

Then he went around again.

Albert made the sandwich,

the egg, and the milk come out even.

Albert sighed. "I like to have
a good lunch," he said.

Frances ate her bread and jam.

Then she went out to the playground and skipped rope.

She did not skip as fast

as she had skipped in the morning,

and she sang:

>Jam in the morning, jam at noon,

>Bread and jam

>By the light of the moon.

>Jam . . . is . . . very . . . nice.

When Frances got home, Mother said,

"I have a snack all ready for you."

"I *do* like snacks!" said Frances.

"Here it is," said Mother.

"A glass of milk

and some nice bread and jam for you."

"Aren't you worried that maybe

I will get sick and all my teeth

will fall out from eating so much

bread and jam?" asked Frances.

"I don't think that will happen

for quite a while," said Mother.

"So eat it all up and enjoy it."

Frances ate up

most of her bread and jam.

But she did not eat all of it.

After her snack

she went outside to skip rope.

Frances skipped a little more slowly
than she had skipped at noon,
and she sang:

> *Jam for snacks and jam for meals,*
> *I know how a jam jar feels—*
> *FULL . . . OF . . . JAM!*

That evening for dinner
Mother cooked spaghetti and meatballs.

"I am glad to see there is enough
for seconds," Father said.
"Because spaghetti and meatballs
is one of my favorite dishes."
"Try a little spaghetti, Gloria,"
said Mother.

Frances looked down at her plate.
There was no spaghetti
and meatballs on it.
There was a slice of bread
and a jar of jam.
Frances began to cry.

"My goodness!" said Mother.

"Frances is crying!"

"What is the matter?" asked Father.

Frances sang a little sad song:

> *What I am*

> *Is tired of jam.*

"I want spaghetti and meatballs,"
said Frances.

"May I have some, please?"

"I had no idea you liked spaghetti
and meatballs!" said Mother.
So Mother gave Frances
spaghetti and meatballs,
and she ate it all up.

The next day

when the bell rang for lunch,

Albert said, "What do you have today?"

"Well," said Frances,

setting a tiny vase of violets

on her desk, "let me see."

41

"I have tomato soup," Frances said.

"And a lobster-salad sandwich.

I have celery, carrot sticks,

and black olives.

And plums, and cherries,

and vanilla pudding."

"That's a good lunch," said Albert.

"I think it's nice that there

are all different kinds of lunches

and breakfasts and dinners and snacks."

"So do I," said Frances,

and she made everything come out even.

The End

For Frances's friends everywhere

BEST FRIENDS
FOR FRANCES

by Russell Hoban

Pictures by Lillian Hoban

It was a fine summer morning,

so Frances took out her bat and ball.

"Will you play ball with me?"

said her little sister, Gloria.

"No," said Frances.

"You are too little."

Gloria sat down and cried.

Frances walked over to her friend

Albert's house, singing a song:

Sisters that are much too small

To throw or catch or bat a ball

Are really not much good at all,

Except for crying.

When Frances got to Albert's house,

he was coming out with

a large brown paper bag.

"Let's play baseball," said Frances.

"I can't," said Albert.

"Today is my wandering day."

"Where do you wander?" said Frances.

"I just go around until I get hungry,"

said Albert. "Then I eat my lunch."

"That's a big lunch," said Frances.

"It's only four or five sandwiches,"
said Albert, "and apples, bananas,
cupcakes, and some chocolate milk."

"Can I wander, too?" said Frances.

"No," said Albert.

"You can't do the things I do
on my wandering days."

"Like what?" said Frances.

"Snake and frog work," said Albert.

"Throwing stones at fences.
Looking for crow feathers."

"I can do all that," said Frances,

"except the snake and frog work."

"That's what I mean," said Albert.

"I'd have to ruin the whole day,
showing you how."

Then Albert went off to wander.

And Frances walked home slowly,

singing:

Fat boys that eat too much lunch

Can't do a thing but munch and crunch

And play with snakes and frogs.

When Frances got home, Gloria said,

"Will you play ball with me now?"

"You can't bat

and you can't catch," said Frances.

"I can if you stand close," said Gloria.

"All right," said Frances,

and she played ball with Gloria.

The next morning,

Frances went to Albert's house.

Albert was playing ball with Harold.

"Can I play?" said Frances.

"She's not much good,"

said Harold to Albert, "and besides,

this is a no-girls game."

"All right," said Frances.
"Then I will go home and play
a no-boys game with Gloria,
Mr. Fat Albert. So ha, ha, ha."
Frances walked home,
and as she walked she sang:
Boys to throw and catch and bat
Are all the friends that Mr. Fat
Albert will have from now on.
He will not have me.

When Frances got home,

Gloria said,

"How did you play so fast?"

"It was a fast game," said Frances.

"You're lucky that you have
a friend to play with," said Gloria.

"I wish I had a friend."

"I thought Ida was your friend,"
said Frances.

"Ida is away at camp," said Gloria,

"and she only plays dolls.

She never wants to catch frogs."

"Can you catch frogs?" said Frances.

"Yes," said Gloria.

"I can show you."

"Later," said Frances.

"Do you want to play ball?"

"All right," said Gloria.

"If any boys come, they can't play,"
said Frances,

"and I think I will

be your friend now."

"How can a sister be a friend?"

said Gloria.

"You'll see," said Frances.

"For frogs and ball and dolls?"

"Yes," said Frances.

"And will you show me how

to print my name?" said Gloria.

"Yes," said Frances.

"Then you will be my best friend,"

said Gloria.

"Will it just be today, or longer?"

"Longer," said Frances.

"And today we will have a picnic.

"There will be songs and games

and prizes.

And no boys," said Frances.

Mother helped Frances and Gloria

get everything ready and packed

in Frances's wagon.

Frances and Gloria set off.

In the wagon were

a picnic lunch in a hamper,

two burlap sacks for the sack race,

an egg for the egg toss,

and a jar with two frogs

for the frog-jumping contest.

Frances made a sign that said:

BEST FRIENDS

OUTING

NO BOYS

They held the sign and Frances sang:

When best friends have an outing,

There are jolly times in store.

There are games and there are prizes,

There is also something more.

There is something in a hamper

That is very good to eat.

When best friends have an outing,

It's a very special treat,

With no boys.

Frances and Gloria

passed Albert's house.

"What's in the hamper?" said Albert,

running out of his house.

"I don't know," said Frances.

"Nothing much.

Hard-boiled eggs and fresh tomatoes.

Carrot and celery sticks.

Some cream cheese-and-jelly

sandwiches, I think.

Salami, pepper-and-egg sandwiches.

Ice-cold root beer, watermelon and

strawberries and cream for dessert.

"There are salt and pepper shakers
and napkins and a checked tablecloth,
which is the way girls do it."
"Could I come along
on the eating?" said Albert.
"You mean outing," said Frances.

"That wagon looks heavy to pull,"
said Albert. "You will get tired
unless I help you."

"I don't know," said Frances.

"You can see from the sign
that this is a no-boys outing.
And it is only for best friends."

"What good is an outing
without boys?" said Albert.

"It is just as good as a ball game
without girls," said Frances,
"and maybe a whole lot better."

"Can I be a best friend?" said Albert.

"I don't think it is the kind of thing
you can do," said Frances.
"And it would ruin my whole day
to have to show you."
"I can do it," said Gloria.
"I can be a best friend,
and I can catch frogs, too."

"I can catch frogs *and* snakes,"
said Albert.

"Let him be a best friend,"
said Gloria.

"And he can show me
how to catch snakes."

"I'll get my snake pillowcase
right now," said Albert.

"Well, I'm not sure," said Frances.

"Maybe you'll be best friends
when it's lunch-in-the-hamper time.
But how about when it's
no-girls-baseball time?"

"When we are best friends,
there won't be no-girls baseball,"
said Albert.
"All right," said Frances.
She crossed out the NO BOYS
on the sign.
Then they started off again.

Albert pulled the wagon,

and Frances and Gloria

carried the sign.

The outing place was at the tree

on the hill by the pond.

First, Albert caught

a snake for Gloria,

and then they played games.

Gloria won the sack race.

Frances won the egg toss.

Albert won the frog-jumping contest

with a fresh frog from the pond.

So everybody won a prize.

Then Frances made up a party song.

And everybody sang it.

When the wasps and the bumblebees

Have a party,

Nobody comes that can't buzz.

When the chicks and ducklings

Have an outing,

Everyone has to wear fuzz.

When the frog and the snake

Have their yearly clambake,

There's plenty

Of wiggling and hopping.

They splash in the pond

And the marshes beyond,

And everyone has to get sopping.

"And at the Best Friends Outing,"

said Albert,

"everyone has to eat, don't they?"

"Yes," said Frances and Gloria.

They opened the hamper.

"I'm not sure we can eat it all,"

said Frances.

"That is what best friends are for,"
said Albert.

And he gave Frances and Gloria a ride
in the wagon, all the way home.

The next day, Albert came over
with a bunch of daisies for Frances.
"What are the daisies for?" she said.
"Well, we are best friends now,
and I am a boy," said Albert.
"That makes me your best boyfriend.
So that is why I brought you daisies."
"Thank you," said Frances.

Then Gloria sat down

on the steps and cried.

"Why are you crying?" said Frances.

"Now you have Albert

to be your best friend," said Gloria.

"And you won't be mine anymore."

"Yes, I will," said Frances.

"And I will give you half the daisies

Albert gave me."

So Frances gave Gloria

half the daisies,

and Gloria stopped crying.

Then Harold came over,

and everybody played baseball—

Gloria too.

For Barbara Alexandra Dicks,
who often signs her name in lower case
but is, in fact, a capital person

A BABY SISTER
FOR FRANCES

by Russell Hoban
Pictures by Lillian Hoban

It was a quiet evening.

Father was reading his newspaper.

Mother was feeding baby Gloria.

Frances was sitting under the sink.

She was singing a little song:

Plinketty, plinketty, plinketty, plink,

Here is the dishrag that's under the

sink.

Here are the buckets and brushes

and me,

Plinketty, plinketty, plinketty, plee.

She stopped the song and listened.

Nobody said anything.

Frances went into her room and took some gravel out of her drawer.

She put the gravel into a coffee can.

She marched into the living room rattling the can and singing:

Here we go marching, rattley bang!

"Please don't do that," said Father.

Frances stopped.

She went back under the sink.

Mother came in, carrying Gloria.

"Why are you sitting under the sink?" said Mother.

"It's cozy," said Frances.

"Would you like to help me put Gloria to bed?" said Mother.

"How much allowance does Gloria get?"

said Frances.

"Only big girls like you

get allowances," said Father.

"May I have a penny with my nickel

now that I am a big sister?"

said Frances.

"Yes," said Father.

"Now you will get six cents a week."

"Thank you," said Frances.

"I know a girl who gets seventeen cents.

She gets three nickels and two pennies."

"Well," said Father, "it's time for bed."

Father picked Frances up

and gave her a piggyback ride to bed.

Mother and Father tucked Frances in
and kissed her good night.

"I need my tiny special blanket,"
said Frances.

Mother gave her the special blanket.

"And I need my tricycle and my sled
and both teddy bears
and my alligator doll," said Frances.

Father brought in the tricycle
and the sled and both teddy bears
and the alligator doll.

Mother and Father kissed her good night
again and Frances went to sleep.

In the morning Frances got up and
washed and began to dress for school.
"Is my blue dress ready for me
to wear?" said Frances.
"Oh, dear," said Mother,
"I was so busy with Gloria
that I did not have time to iron it,
so you'll have to wear the yellow one."
Mother buttoned Frances up the back.
Then she brushed her hair
and put a new ribbon in it
and put her breakfast on the table.

"Why did you put sliced bananas
on the oatmeal?" said Frances.
"Did you forget that I like raisins?"
"No, I did not forget," said Mother,
"but you finished up the raisins
yesterday and I have not been out
shopping yet."

"Well," said Frances, "things are not very good around here anymore.

No clothes to wear.

No raisins for the oatmeal.

I think maybe I'll run away."

"Finish your breakfast," said Mother.

"What time will dinner be tonight?" said Frances.

"Half past six," said Mother.

"Then I will have time to run away after dinner," said Frances,
and she kissed her mother good-bye and went to school.

After dinner that evening
Frances packed her little knapsack
very carefully.
She put in her tiny special blanket
and her alligator doll.
She took all of the nickels and pennies
out of her bank, for travel money,
and she took her good luck coin
for good luck.
Then she took a box of prunes
from the kitchen
and five chocolate sandwich cookies.

"Well," said Frances, "it is time
to say good-bye.
I am on my way. Good-bye."
"Where are you running away to?"
said Father.
"I think that under the dining-room
table is the best place," said Frances.
"It's cozy, and the kitchen is near
if I run out of cookies."
"That is a good place to run away to,"
said Mother, "but I'll miss you."
"I'll miss you too," said Father.

"Well," said Frances, "good-bye,"
and she ran away.

Father sat down with his newspaper.

Mother took up her knitting.

"You know, it is not the same house without Frances," said Father.

"That is *exactly* what I was thinking," said Mother.

"The place seems empty without her."

Frances sat under the dining-room table and ate her prunes.

"Even Gloria can feel it," said Mother.

"A girl looks up to a big sister."

"I can hear her crying a little right now," said Father.

Father picked up his newspaper.

Then he put it down again.

"I miss the songs that Frances

used to sing," he said.

"I was *so* fond of those little songs,"

said Mother.

"Do you remember the one

about the tomato?

'What does the tomato say,

early in the dawn?'" sang Mother.

"'Time to be all red again,

now that night is gone,'" sang Father.

"Yes," he said, "that is a good one,

but my favorite has always been:

'When the wasps and the bumblebees

have a party, nobody comes that can't

buzz. . . .'"

"Well," said Mother, "we shall just have

to get used to a quiet house now."

Frances ate three sandwich cookies
and put the other two aside for later.
She began to sing:

I am poor and hungry here,

eating prunes and rice.

Living all alone is not

really very nice.

She had no rice,
but chocolate sandwich cookies
did not sound right for the song.

"I can almost hear her now," said Father,
humming the tune that Frances
had just sung.

"She has a charming voice."

"It is just not a *family* without Frances,"
said Mother.

"Babies are very nice.
Goodness knows I *like* babies,
but a baby is not a family."

"Isn't that a fact!" said Father.

"A family is *everybody all together*."

"Think how lucky Gloria is to have
a sister like Frances," said Mother.

"I agree," said Father,
"and I hope that Gloria turns out to be
as clever and good as Frances."

"With a big sister like Frances,
she will turn out fine," said Mother.

"I'd like to hear from Frances,"
said Father, "just to know how she is."

"I'd like to hear from Frances too,"
said Mother, "and I'm not sure
the sleeves are right on this sweater
I'm knitting for her."

"Hello," called Frances

from the dining room.

"I am calling on the telephone.

Hello, hello, this is me.

Is that you?"

"Hello," said Mother.

"This is us.

How are you?"

"I am fine," said Frances.

"This is a nice place,

but you miss your family

when you're away.

How are you?"

"We are all well," said Father,

"but we miss you too."

"I will be home soon," said Frances,

and she hung up.

"Frances said that she will be home
soon," said Father.

"I think I'll bake a cake," said Mother.

Frances put on her knapsack and sang
a little traveling song:

Big sisters really have to stay

At home, not travel far away,

Because everybody misses them

And wants to hug-and-kisses them.

"I'm not sure about that last rhyme,"
said Frances as she arrived
in the living room.

"That's a good enough rhyme,"
said Father.
"I like it fine," said Mother,
and they both hugged and kissed her.

"What kind of cake are you baking?"
said Frances to Mother.

"Chocolate," said Mother.

"It's too bad that Gloria's too little
to have some," said Frances,

"but when she's a big girl like me,
she can have chocolate cake too."

"Oh, yes," said Mother,

"you may be sure that
there will always be plenty
of chocolate cake around here."

The End

for Lynn Klotz
who would certainly give
her little sister a Chompo Bar
if she had a little sister

A BIRTHDAY
FOR FRANCES

by Russell Hoban
Pictures by Lillian Hoban

It was the day before

Frances's little sister Gloria's birthday.

Mother and Gloria were making

place cards for the party.

Frances was in the closet, singing:

Happy Thursday to you,

Happy Thursday to you,

Happy Thursday, dear Alice,

Happy Thursday to you.

"Who is Alice?" asked Mother.

"Alice is somebody that nobody

can see," said Frances.

"That is why she has no birthday.

I am singing Happy Thursday to her."

"Today is Friday," said Mother.

"It is Thursday for Alice," said Frances.

"Alice will not have h-r-n-d."

"What is h-r-n-d?" asked Mother.

"Cake. I thought you could spell.
Alice will not have cake because
she does not have a birthday,"
said Frances.

"Alice has one birthday every year,
and so do you," said Mother.

"Your birthday is in two months.

Then you will be the birthday girl.

But tomorrow is Gloria's birthday."

"That is how it is, Alice," said Frances.

"Your birthday is always the one

that is not now."

"Wouldn't you and Alice like to come

out of the broom closet and help

me make place cards?" said Mother.

"What are you drawing?" Frances asked.

"Pretty flowers," said Gloria.

"Rainbows and happy trees."

Frances began to draw and sing:

A rainbow and a happy tree

Are not for Alice or for me.

I will draw three-legged cats.

And caterpillars with ugly hats.

Frances stopped singing.

"Gloria kicked me under the table,"

said Frances.

"Mean Frances," said Gloria.

"Gloria is mean," said Frances.

"Gloria hid my pail and my shovel."

"That was last year," said Mother.

"When Gloria is mean,
it was always last year," said Frances.

"But me and Alice know s-m-f-o."

"What is s-m-f-o?" asked Mother.

"Better," said Frances. "Good-bye.

I will be out of town visiting Alice."

Frances went to the broom closet

and took out her favorite broom.

"Let's go, Champ," she said.

"I'm ready to ride."

Frances was riding back and forth

on her broom on the porch, and as she

rode she sang a song for Alice:

Everybody makes a fuss

For birthday girls who are not us.

Girls who take your pail away

Eat cake and q-p-m all day.

"Is q-p-m ice cream?" Mother asked.

"Yes," said Frances.

Frances climbed up on one of

the porch rocking chairs

and looked through the window

at the boxes Mother was wrapping.

"What is Gloria getting from you

and from Father for her birthday?"

asked Frances.

"A paintbox and a tea set
and a plush pig," said Mother.

"I am not going to give Gloria
any present," said Frances.

"That is all right," said Mother,
and Frances began to cry.

"What is the matter?" said Mother.

"Everybody is giving Gloria
a present but me," said Frances.

"Would you like to give Gloria
a present?" said Mother.

"Yes," said Frances.

"If I had my next two allowances,
I would have a nickel and two pennies
and another nickel and two pennies,
and I could buy a Chompo Bar and
four balls of bubble gum for Gloria."

"I think it is very nice of you

to want to give Gloria

a birthday present," said Mother,

and she gave Frances

her next two allowances.

That evening Father took Frances

to the candy store

to buy a Chompo Bar

and four balls of bubble gum

for Gloria.

As they walked home

Frances said to Father,

"Are you sure that it is all right

for Gloria to have a whole Chompo Bar?

Maybe she is too young

for that kind of candy.

Maybe it will make her sick."

"Well," said Father, "I do not think

it would be good for Gloria to eat

Chompo Bars every day.

But tomorrow is her birthday,

and I think it will be

all right for her to eat one."

Frances thought about Gloria
and the Chompo Bar,
and while she thought she put two
of the bubble-gum balls into her mouth
without noticing it.

Frances chewed the bubble gum
and squeezed the Chompo Bar a little.
"Chompo Bars have nougat, caramel,
chocolate, and nuts," said Frances.

"Probably Gloria could not eat
more than half of one."
"I'm sure that Gloria could eat
the whole Chompo Bar," said Father.
"That is why it is such a good present."
"Yes," said Frances,
"and I spent two allowances on Gloria."
Frances put the other two gum balls
into her mouth and sang:
Chompo Bars are nice to get.
Chompo Bars taste better yet
When they're someone else's.
"You would not eat Gloria's Chompo Bar,
would you?" said Father.
"It is not Gloria's yet," said Frances.

"I can hardly understand

what you are saying," said Father.

"Is there something in your mouth?"

"I think maybe there is bubble gum,"

said Frances, "but I don't remember

how it got there."

"Maybe I should take care of

the Chompo Bar until you are ready

to give it to Gloria," said Father.

"All right," said Frances,

and she gave the Chompo Bar

to Father to take care of.

The next day was Gloria's birthday,
and the party was that afternoon.

The cake was ready,

the table was all set,

and Mother was making hot chocolate.

There were little baskets of gum drops

and chocolate-covered peanuts

for everybody.

There were place cards

and party poppers

for Mother and Father,

for Frances and Gloria,

for Gloria's friend Ida,

and for Frances's friend Albert.

Albert was the first friend to arrive,
and he and Frances sat down
while they were waiting for Ida.
"What are you giving Gloria?"
Frances asked Albert.
"A little tiny truck," said Albert.

"I am thinking of giving Gloria

a Chompo Bar," said Frances.

"But I am not sure.

I might and I might not.

I had to spend almost two

whole allowances on it."

"That's how it is," said Albert.

"I had to spend my allowance money

on my sister when she had a birthday."

"Little sisters are not much r-v-s-m,"

said Frances.

"Good?" said Albert.

"That's right," said Frances.

"No, they are not," said Albert.

"Little sisters can't catch
or throw," said Albert.
"They take your sand pail
and your shovel too," said Frances.

"I don't think many of them deserve
a Chompo Bar."

"Here is Ida now," said Mother,

"and the party can begin."

"When are the presents?" said Gloria.

"First," said Father, "your mother

will bring out the cake,

and I will light the candles.

We will sing 'Happy Birthday to You.'

Then you make a wish.

Then you get your presents."

"I know what to wish," said Gloria.

"Don't tell it," said Ida.

"It won't come true if you do,"
said Albert.

"Here comes the cake," said Mother.

She put it on the table,
and Father lit the candles.

Then everybody sang
"Happy Birthday to You."

Frances did not sing the words
that the others were singing.
Very softly, so that nobody
could hear her, she sang:
Happy Chompo to me
Is how it ought to be—
Happy Chompo to Frances,
Happy Chompo to me.
"Make your wish and blow out
the candles," said Mother to Gloria.
"I want to tell my wish," said Gloria.
"No, no!" said Mother and Father
and Frances and Albert and Ida.

"Just say it inside your head,"
said Albert.
Gloria said her wish inside her head
and blew out the candles at once.
"Hooray!" said everybody.

"Now your wish will come true,"
said Mother.

"This is what I wished," said Gloria:
"I wished that Frances would be nice
and not be mad at me
because I hid her sand pail
and shovel last year.
And I am sorry, and I will be nice."

"She told," said Ida.

"Now her wish won't come true."

"I think it will come true,"
said Mother, "because it is
a special kind of good wish
that can make itself come true."

153

"Well," said Frances to Gloria,

"I think your wish will come true too.

And I have a present for you,

and I owe you four balls

of bubble gum."

"Now it is time for the presents?"

said Gloria.

"Yes," said Father.

Father and Mother gave Gloria

the paintbox and the tea set

and the plush pig.

Albert gave her the little tiny truck.

Ida gave her a little china baby doll.

Frances had wrapped the Chompo Bar

in pretty paper

and tied it with a ribbon,

and now she got ready to give it to Gloria.

"What is it?" asked Gloria.

"It is something good to eat,"

said Frances,

"and I will give it to you in a minute.

But first I will sing

'Happy Birthday to You,'

because I did not really sing it before.

Happy birthday to you," sang Frances,

and she squeezed the Chompo Bar.

"Happy birthday to you."

Then she stopped

and rested a little.

"You can have a bite when I get it,"

said Gloria.

157

Frances took a deep breath

and finished the song,

"Happy birthday, dear Gloria,

happy birthday to you.

Here," said Frances.

She squeezed the Chompo Bar

one last time and gave it to Gloria.

"You can eat it all, because

you are the birthday girl," said Frances.

"Thank you," said Gloria

as she unwrapped the Chompo Bar.

"This is a good present."

And she ate it all,

because she was the birthday girl.